Commander Toad PaperStars from Jane Yolen and Bruce Degen

COMMANDER TOAD IN SPACE
COMMANDER TOAD AND THE PLANET OF THE GRAPES
COMMANDER TOAD AND THE BIG BLACK HOLE
COMMANDER TOAD AND THE DIS-ASTEROID
COMMANDER TOAD AND THE INTERGALACTIC SPY
COMMANDER TOAD AND THE SPACE PIRATES

COMMANDER TOAD
and the
SPACE PIRATES

by JANE YOLEN

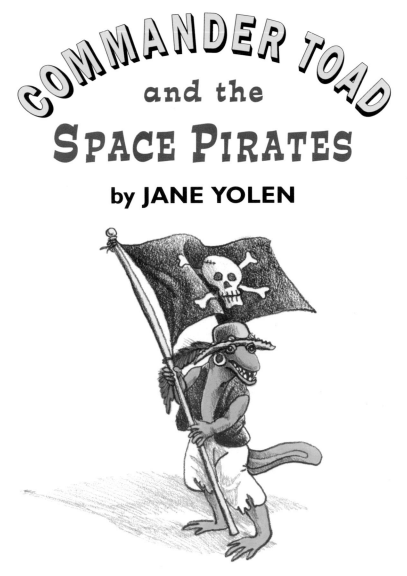

pictures by BRUCE DEGEN

The Putnam & Grosset Group

Library of Congress Cataloging-in-Publication Data
Yolen, Jane. Commander Toad and the space pirates.
Summary: When Commander Salamander and his band of pirates
capture the "Star Wars" spaceship, Commander Toad is forced
to hop the plank. [1. Toads—Fiction. 2. Pirates—Fiction.
3. Science Fiction.] I. Degen, Bruce, ill. II. Title.
PZ7.Y78CNS 1987 [E] 86-32748
ISBN 0-698-11419-1
13 15 17 19 20 18 16 14 12

To David, Heidi, Adam, and Jason
who suffered through all the puns—
and Andrew who supplied a few of them.
—JY

For Art Greenberg, Bernie Rattiner and
Ann Teicher, whose kindness and
understanding to this Space Cadet,
have been out of this world.
—BD

Long green ships
fly through space,
deep and dark
and silent space.
There is one ship,
long and green,
a green machine,
called *Star Warts*.
The captain of this ship
is Commander Toad,
brave and bright,
bright and brave.

There is no one like him
in all the fleet.
He guides his ship
where no space ship
has gone before.
To find planets.
To explore galaxies.
To bring a little bit of Earth
out to the alien stars.

Commander Toad
has a really fine crew.
His copilot is
Mr. Hop.
His master of machines is
Lieutenant Lily.
His computer chief is
young Jake Skyjumper.

And the doctor
who keeps everybody
hoppy and well is
old Doc Peeper
in his grass-green wig.

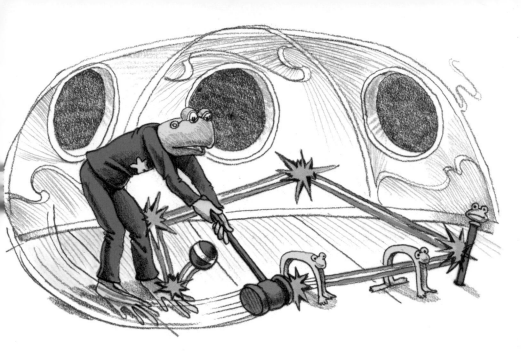

It has been a long trip
and a boring trip.
Nothing has happened.
The crew has played
lots of games.
They have played
leapfrog
and hopscotch
and croak-kay
thirty-five times each.
They are tired of games.

They have read
lots and lots of books.
They have read
Robin Toad,
and *The Lizard of Oz,*
and *Snow White*
and the Seven Warts
forty-seven times each.
They are tired of books.

They have watched
lots and lots and lots
of movies.
They have watched
Splash Gordon,
and *The Toad Warrior,*
and *Indiana Frog*
and the Lily Pad of Doom
fifty-nine times each.
They are tired of movies.

"There is nothing to do,"
says young Jake.
"I sure would like
an adventure."
He yawns.
"Life on a space ship
is boring, boring, boring."

"You could clean up
this mess,"
says Commander Toad,
pointing to a pile
of boxes and bags.
"All of you
can help.
Then no one will be bored."

But Mr. Hop
and Lieutenant Lily
and old Doc Peeper
are fast asleep.
There is only
Jake Skyjumper
to do the job.
He starts to stack
boxes and bags
when . . .

Aaaaa-OOOOO-ga!
Aaaaa-OOOOO-ga!
It is the ship's alarm.
Everyone hops
to a battle station.
Young Jake cries out,
"Look on the screen.
There is a ship
heading toward us.
I do not like its looks."

18

They all peer out
the portholes.
There is a black ship
coming toward them.
A black ship
with a white skull
and white crossbones
painted on its side.

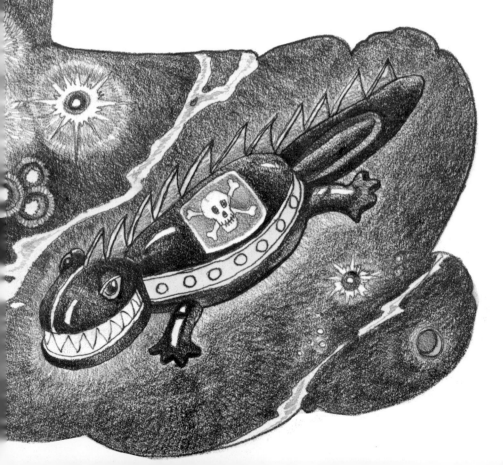

"Quick," says
Commander Toad,
"I recognize that ship.
It is my old enemy
Commander Salamander.
He has been called
Scourge of the Skies,
Goon of the Galaxies,
the Snake of Outer Space.
He is ugly, green,
and very mean.

We must reverse engines
and get out
while the getting out
can be got."
"But what about being
brave and bright,
bright and brave?"
asks Lieutenant Lily.
"What about guns
and glory?"

Commander Toad
does not hear her.
He is too busy
with the engines,
and the buttons,
and the levers,
and the pulleys.

"Commander Toad
believes in running
instead of gunning,"
explains Mr. Hop.
"Especially when
your old enemy
has many more guns
than you do."
He points to the black ship
which has guns everywhere.

But it is too late to run.
The pirate ship
holds *Star Warts*
in its tractor beams.
A strange ladder
shoots out
and clamps onto
Star Warts' side.

Across that ladder
come the pirates,
slithering,
sliding,
whooping,
hopping,
and looking as wicked
as can be.

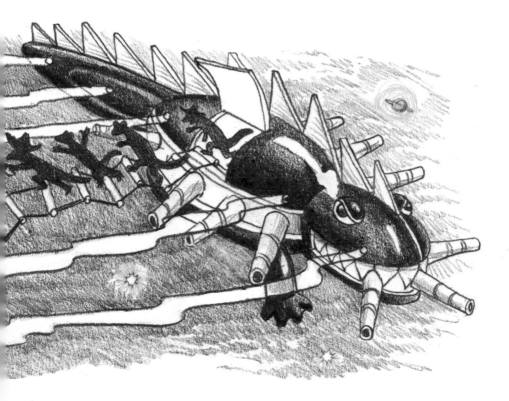

The door whooshes open
and in they come.
At their head
is their slimy chief.
He twirls his mustaches
and shouts,
"Yo-ho-ho, me warties!
I am Commander Salamander.
I am ugly, green,
and very mean!"
"I told you,"
whispers Commander Toad.

The pirate chief keeps shouting.
"Some call me
Scourge of the Skies.
Some call me
Goon of the Galaxies.
Some call me
The Snake of Outer Space.
But *you* can call me sir!"
"Yes sir!" shout his toadies.
They snarl
at the *Star Warts* crew.

"And you can call me sir, too,"
says Commander Salamander,
twirling his mustaches
and grinning.
"No we won't,"
says Commander Toad.
"No matter what you do."

"Absolutely not,"
says Lieutenant Lily.
"Never!" says young Jake,
though his voice squeaks.
Mr. Hop says nothing
but he is thinking
dark thoughts
behind his green face.

And what of old Doc Peeper?
He is hiding
behind the boxes and bags
that Jake piled up,
boxes and bags
filled with
bandages
and splints
and a whole lot of
tongue depressors.

"You refuse to call me *sir?*
How boring,"
says Commander Salamander.
"That is what they all say—
at first."
He twirls his mustaches
and yawns loudly.
His men yawn, too,
one after another,
after another,
after another,
after another,
after another.

"And do you know what I do
when I am bored?"
asks Commander Salamander.
One of his men,
all slithers and slime,
with a patch over one eye,
raises his hand.
"Do you read books?"
he asks.
Commander Salamander
shakes his head.
"Boring," he says.

33

Another pirate,
all feathers and fangs,
with a great gold earring,
raises his tail.
"Do you watch movies?"
"Double boring,"
says Commander Salamander.
A third pirate,

all tentacles and talons,
raises his eyebrow.
"I know, I know,"
he says with a wicked grin.
"You play games."
Commander Salamander
twirls his mustaches.
He smiles, too.
It is not a nice smile.

"I do not play leapfrog,"
says Commander Salamander.
"And I do not play croak-kay.
I play . . ."
The pirates all smile.

These are not nice smiles.
They jump up and down
and shout together,
"Hop the Plank!
You play Hop the Plank."
"Right! Ahoy!
And yo-ho-ho!
That is what *I* play!"
says Commander Salamander.

"What does he mean?"
asks Lieutenant Lily.
But Commander Toad
does not answer.
He puts his hand
to his forehead
and whispers,
"Hop the Plank."
Then he sits down
heavily
in his captain's chair.

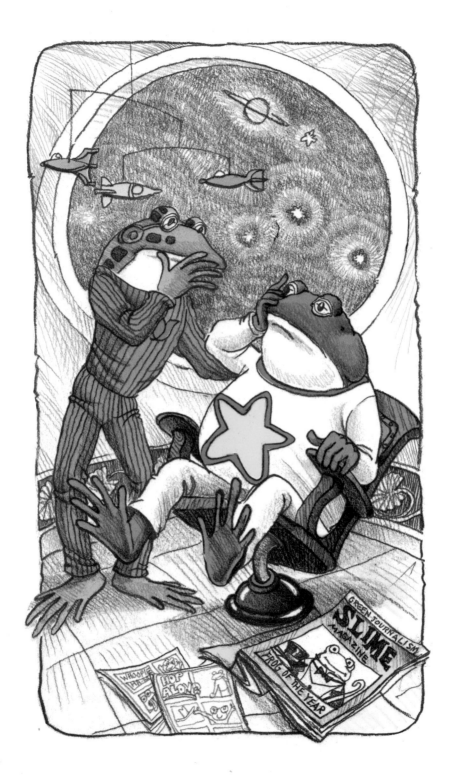

The pirates
set to work.
They tie up
Commander Toad.
They tie up
Lieutenant Lily.
They tie up
Mr. Hop.
They tie up
young Jake Skyjumper
right in front of the computer.

They do not tie up
old Doc Peeper
because he is
still hiding
behind the boxes
and behind the bags
bandages,
and splints,
and a whole lot of
tongue depressors.

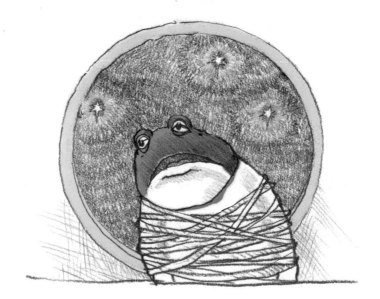

All the pirates
punch each other
on the shoulders,
and pound each other
on the backs,
and pinch each other
on the tails
and laugh.
Commander Salamander
laughs the loudest.
Then he claps his hands.
"MAKE THE PLANK!"

The pirates take
boards out of the bunk beds
and tie them together.
"Plank ready, sir!"
Commander Salamander
claps his hands again.
"TAKE THE PLANK!"
The pirates
pick up the plank
and take it to the door.

Commander Salamander
claps his hands
a third time.
"FAKE THE PLANK!"
The pirates balance
the plank on their knees.
They put Commander Toad
on one end
and tie a scarf
around his eyes.

45

They shout
"HOP! HOP! HOPPITY HOP!"
and push Commander Toad
from the back.
Commander Toad
falls down.
He bumps his nose
on the floor.
It does not make him
very hoppy.

"Now listen,"
says Commander Salamander
to the other members
of the *Star Warts* crew.
"If you do not
co-hoperate,
you will *all* have to
hop the plank.
You will not hop it
inside your ship.
You will hop it

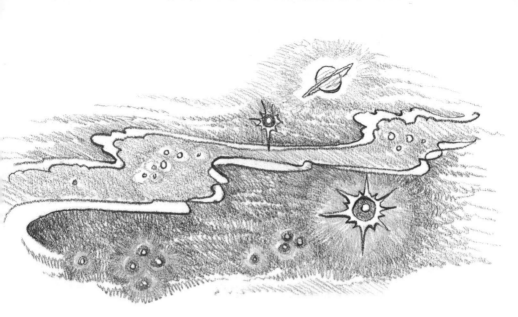

outside your ship.
You will not bump
your noses
on the floor
because there will be
no floor out there
to bump your noses on.
You will spin
and spin
and spin forever
out in deep hopper space."

He twirls his mustaches
and he laughs.
It is a very wicked laugh.
Commander Toad
looks grim.
Lieutenant Lily
looks angry.
Mr. Hop
looks thoughtful.
And young Jake Skyjumper
looks scared.

No one knows
how old Doc Peeper looks
in his grass-green wig,
for he is hiding
behind the boxes and bags
filled with
bandages,
and splints,
and a whole lot of
tongue depressors.

"Now me slimys,"
Commander Salamander
says to his pirates,
"let's see what
this starship
has for us to take."
They peek
into the pantry.
They poke
into the closets.
They push
into the bedrooms.

They make a big mess
and a lot of noise.
"Yo-ho-ho,
me slithery-slees,"
cries Commander Salamander.
"No mothers here
to make us clean up.
No fathers here
to make us shut up.
No captains
or commanders here
to make us give up.
Now what should we do?"

The pirates look around.
There is nothing more
to mess up.
And nothing more
to tear up.
Except a big stack
of boxes and bags
filled with
bandages,
and splints,
and a whole lot of
tongue depressors.
They rush over to it.

Suddenly,
from behind the pile,
something big appears.
Something wrapped in
white bandages
with sticks for arms
and a grass-green wig
on top of its head.
It looks like a mummy.
It walks like a mummy.
It talks like a mummy.

"Clean up this mess,"
says the mummy,
"or no cookies for you."
It claps its long arms.
It whacks one pirate
on the rear.
"Yes, Mummy,"
says the pirate.
It smacks one pirate
on the ear.
"Right away, Mummy,"
says the pirate.

It cracks
Commander Salamander
on the tail.
"Anything you say, Mummy."
The pirates slither
and slide,
and whoop,
and hop to work.

Soon the *Star Warts*
is shipshape again.
While they are cleaning,
the mummy is busy, too.
It cuts all the ropes
tying up the crew.

Commander Toad
and his crew
leap up
and one-two-three
they capture
all the pirates.
Even Commander Salamander,
who twirls his mustaches
so hard
one side falls off.

Commander Toad laughs
and pulls off the other side.
Commander Salamander laughs.
"Now *that*
was some adventure,"
says Commander Toad.
He rubs his nose,
which still hurts
just a little
from hopping the plank.
"Welcome aboard,
my old friend Sally.
Come and meet
my no-longer-bored crew."

61

"You mean
this was all a joke,"
says young Jake.
Commander Toad smiles.
"Star Fleet
likes to keep its crews
in tip-top shape."
Commander Salamander smiles.
"In tip-top shape
and hip-hop shape."

He rubs *under* his nose
where the mustaches
used to be.
"Can we trade
books and movies?"
he asks Commander Toad.
So they trade
and trade.
Each crew has many
brand new books
and brand new movies.
They are no longer bored.

The pirates go
back to their own ship,
singing and waving.
"Good-by, good-by,"
the crew of *Star Warts*
calls out.
"Now put her into
hopper drive,"
says Commander Toad.
And then they
leapfrog
across the galaxy
from star
to star
to star.